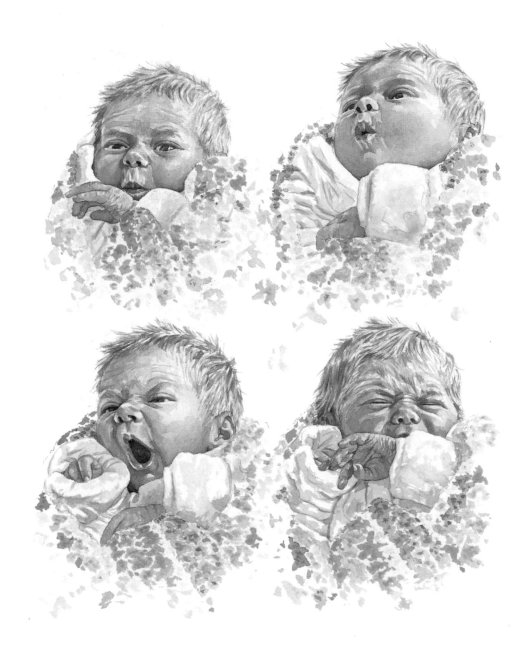

For Gabriel Finn and the Dolphins, Kia and Teagan
—*C.B.*

First published in the United States by Dial Books
A division of Penguin Putnam Inc.
345 Hudson Street, New York, New York 10014
Published in Great Britain by Frances Lincoln Limited

Printed in Hong Kong
First Edition
1 3 5 7 9 10 8 6 4 2

Library of Congress Cataloging in Publication Data
Henderson, Kathy, date.
Newborn/ by Kathy Henderson; pictures by Caroline Binch.—1st ed.
p. cm.
Summary: A newborn baby experiences the sights, sounds,
and sensations of life and the whole wide world.
ISBN 0-8037-2434-9
[1. Babies—Fiction.] I. Binch, Caroline, ill. II. Title.
PZ7.H8305Ne   1999
[E]—dc21   98-33674   CIP   AC

The full-color artwork was prepared using pencil and watercolor.

Newborn

KATHY HENDERSON ◇ CAROLINE BINCH

DIAL BOOKS ◇ NEW YORK

Welcome, little baby,
newborn and just waking.
Lie close in my arms
and I'll show you the world.

Look, there are shadows
of daylight and darkness
scattered and dappled all over the wall.

And that's your warm blanket
that's tickling and teasing
your sleepy soft cheek.

And there—
those strange things
waving around in the air
are your fingers,
and that stuff they're tangling is hair.

Here, little baby,
the light swings and turns
as you ride through the house.

There are colors
and noises,
the tumble of voices,
a creak and a bang
as a bedroom door slams.

There is rustling, crackling,
paper unwrapping,
the click of a switch
and a whistling, flickering
picture that speaks.

And then there's the wind
that rattles and moans,
and the startle-stop, startle-stop call
of the telephone.

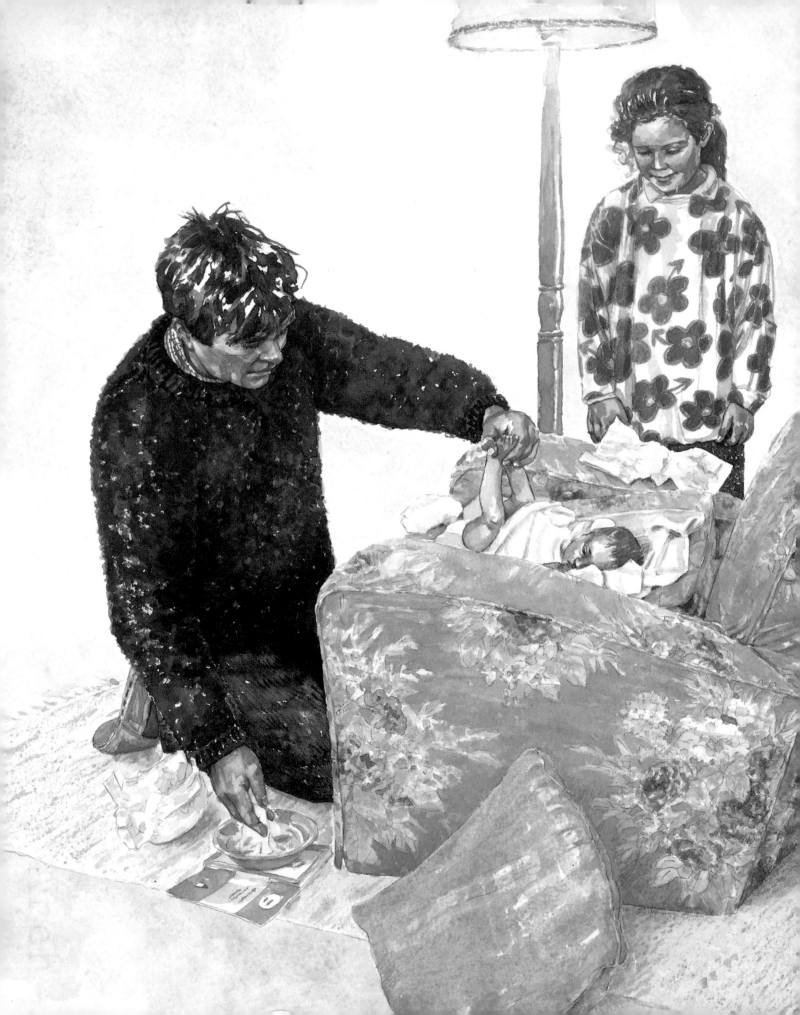

Come, little baby, we'll sit down here.
This is a table
and this is a chair
and that's a lightbulb glowing there.

And that colored shape
is the wing of a flower,
and that snaky line
is a strand of white string.

And there's the ring of the bell at the door,
and here's Aunt Ella bringing you more,
even more flowers.

And this is the fur
and the tail and the whiskers,
this is the purr of the fireside cat.

And now you hear laughter,
your brother is teasing,
and *a-a-a-WHOO-SHOO!*
your father is sneezing.

And those sounds are music—
look, you can dance too,
and there, that's a mirror,
and that baby's you.

Here, little baby, look up high.
This is a window,
and out there's the sky
and the sun and the wind
and the rain and the clouds
and cars and people and houses and lights,
and at night there are stars—
there's the whole universe.

And this?
It's the edge of the curtain flapping,
blue cloth with patterns.

And this is a hug,
and this is a kiss,
and this is your blanket,
and here's your warm cradle.

Sleep, little baby,
who knows what you've seen
or what worlds you dream of,
so small and newborn.